ISBN 0-86163-461-6

This edition first published 1993 by
Award Publications Limited,
27 Longford Street, London NW1 3DZ

Reprinted 1995

Printed in Italy

THE RIVER BANK

from Kenneth Grahame's
THE WIND IN THE WILLOWS

Adapted by Jane Carruth

Illustrated by Rene Cloke

AWARD PUBLICATIONS

Mole had been very busy all the morning spring-cleaning his little house.

He had swept the floor with his big broom, dusted the table and chairs with his yellow duster and now he was using up all his whitewash on the walls.

"Bother all this spring-cleaning!" Mole said aloud. "I've had enough!"

And he stopped working and bolted down the narrow dark tunnel that led into the fields above his little underground home.

“This is the life for me!” Mole cried, as he trotted through the sweet-scented grass. “All that dusting and cleaning is not good for a fellow!”

Mole was so happy that he sang a little song as he made his way along the side of the hedge, and he did a little dance.

It was a lovely day and Mole decided to stay away from home for a long time. He wandered through one meadow and then into the next until — quite suddenly — he came upon the river.

Mole had never seen the river before and he sat down on the grassy bank to look at it.

After a time he caught sight of a brown little face with whiskers looking at him from a dark hole in the opposite bank. Then Mole saw the whole of him. It was Ratty, the Water Rat!

"Hello, Mole," called Ratty. "How would you like to pay me a visit? I'll come over and fetch you in my boat."

"I'd like it very much," Mole called back.

Ratty wasted no time. He jumped into his boat and began rowing himself across the river. It took him only minutes to reach the other side.

"I've never been in a boat before," Mole confessed, as he climbed into the boat. "But I'm sure I'll like it..."

"Then we'll make a day of it," Ratty cried. "We'll have a picnic."

Ratty rowed the boat back to his landing-stage. He tied up and climbed into his hole. When he came out he was carrying a big heavy picnic basket.

As soon as Ratty was sure Mole was quite comfortable he took up the oars. "We'll make for the old water mill," he said, "even though we'll have to pass the Wild Wood..."

"I've not heard of the Wild Wood," Mole said, without much curiosity.

"Just as well," exclaimed Ratty. "The weasels and ferrets live there and most of them are downright wicked..."

He said no more about the weasels for he was busy steering his boat alongside the river bank so that they could land and set out their picnic.

Ratty spread the picnic things on the grass close to the water mill and Mole sighed.

It was not a SAD sigh but a very happy sigh!

It was one of the best days of his life! There was so much to eat he didn't know what to try first…

As they lay in the sun, Ratty and Mole talked about all the things they enjoyed most and Mole began to feel he had known Ratty all his life.

He was just about to say so when, without warning, a wet and furry head popped out of the water.

It was Otter!

"Well, I never!" Otter cried, climbing on to the bank. "You greedy beggars! You should have invited me to your picnic, Ratty. Why didn't you?"

To Mole's amazement, Otter began helping himself to the rest of the food. He gobbled up everything within reach before Ratty could stop him.

When Otter saw there was nothing much left, he wiped his paws on his whiskers.

"Everybody seems to be out on the river today," he remarked presently.

"We haven't seen anybody," Ratty said. "That is apart from yourself..."

"Well, Toad is out for one. He's in his brand new boat and he's wearing his smart new boating clothes..."

Just then Toad flashed into view, rowing as hard as he could. Ratty waved to him excitedly, but Toad just shook his head and rowed on.

"I-I don't think I have had the pleasure of ever meeting Mr. Toad," said Mole somewhat shyly. "He seems a very important person."

"He thinks he is," said Water Rat shortly. "He certainly thinks he is!"

"If you ask me," said Otter loudly, "he's no more important than that old Mother Rabbit you see up there on the bank. I just know for a fact that she has a huge family to feed...!"

Mole didn't know what to say to this. Up till now he had not had much use for rabbits.

Just then Toad came back into view. He was clearly enjoying himself.

“It would be nice if you could meet Toad,” Water Rat exclaimed. And he scrambled to his feet and began waving frantically, making all kinds of signals to Toad to come ashore.

“I wouldn’t waste your time,” said Otter, as Toad rowed on, with scarcely a backward glance towards the bank. “He just wants to show off his new boat…”

Mole and Ratty were now beginning to feel very sleepy but not Master Otter. He was still hungry!

"I tell you what..." he began, and then broke off. He had seen a big fat mayfly, and with scarcely a splash, he dived into the water after it.

"This has been the best day of my life," Mole said with feeling, when Ratty at last said it was time to go home.

Mole helped Ratty pack away what was left of their picnic and they were soon on the river.

As they glided along, Mole suddenly cried, “Ratty! Ratty! Let me row! I must…” And he jumped up and grabbed the oars, knocking Ratty backwards, off his seat.

“Stop it, you idiot!” Rat shouted. “You’ll have us both in the water!”

He was too late. Into the river they both went with a mighty SPLASH!

Mole spluttered and choked as the water closed over his head. But Ratty was a fine swimmer and went to his rescue, bringing him to the bank.

Then he dived into the river again to recover the boat and fish up the basket.

Mole was so ashamed of himself that all he could say was, “I’m sorry, Ratty. Can you ever forgive me?”

“Of course I can!” Ratty said cheerfully.

"It was all rather fun, you know! Now be a good fellow and cheer up!"

Mole was so touched by Ratty's kind words that he brushed away a tear with his paw and Rat pretended not to notice.

"I tell you what," he said at last. "Why don't you come home with me, Mole, and stay for a few days. I'll teach you to swim and to row and we'll have a jolly time."

"There is nothing — absolutely nothing in the whole world I would like better," Mole said, with great feeling.

"That's settled then," Ratty cried, as he helped Mole into the boat and took up the oars. "We'll be home soon and you can dry off properly."

As soon as they reached home, Ratty insisted Mole wear his best smoking-jacket. Then he made a good fire in the parlour and produced a very tasty supper.

As he sat in front of the roaring fire, with a mug of warm milky tea in his hand, Mole felt completely at home. He said as much to Ratty who immediately began making plans for the next day.

"What do you say we go to Toad Hall," he suggested, "and visit Mr. Toad?"

"What a splendid idea!" Mole cried. "I would love to meet Mr. Toad and see Toad Hall for myself…"

"And so you shall," said Rat smiling. "You won't be disappointed in Toad Hall," he went on, "for it's the grandest house for miles around and very big…"

"I-I do hope I won't be too ordinary for your Mr. Toad," Mole said shyly.

"Of course you won't," Ratty declared. "We'll set out first thing in the morning."

After more talk about Toad Hall, Rat took Mole to the spare room and wished him a very good sleep. "Don't forget," he said, "you can stay here as long as you like."

They set out early the next morning by boat. "You'll see Toad Hall round the next bend in the river," Rat said.

Mole was quite overcome at the sight of the large handsome brick house. "My, my!" he kept saying.

Ratty smiled to himself as he steered his boat to Toad's landing-stage and made her fast. Then he helped Mole to step ashore.

The smooth green lawns went right down to the water's edge and presently Ratty and Mole found themselves strolling along between banks of bright flowers.

"Look, there he is!" Ratty cried suddenly. "There is Toad himself!"

Toad was sitting in a wicker basket-chair when he caught sight of the two friends and he dropped the large map he was studying and cried, "Hooray! How splendid! I was just going to send for you, Ratty!"

"Don't get too excited, Toady," Water Rat said quietly. "This is my friend Mole come to visit you…"

"I need you both," Toad said more calmly. "You are the very animals I want to see…"

"Is it about rowing?" Ratty asked.

"Come and see!" cried Toad.

Toad took the two friends into the stable-yard and there — shining and new, and painted a bright yellow and green with red wheels — stood a Gypsy caravan!

"Well," said Toad, trying hard not to look pleased with himself. "Who wants a life on the open road? This is the finest caravan ever built — and it belongs to me!"

Mole had never seen anything so grand in his life and he said so which meant Toad loved him on sight!

"Come inside my dear fellow," Toad said. "You too, Ratty."

"I'll stay on the step," Ratty said, and it was clear to Mole that he was not really very impressed.

"Look," said Toad, ignoring Ratty. "It's all complete for a long journey. All the stores you could want…"

"Wonderful, wonderful!" Mole said, over and over again.

Ratty said nothing as Toad asked Mole to inspect the shelves and lockers all crammed with tins and bottles, and jars of delicious jams and pickles.

"I've planned everything!" Toad cried. "We are ready to start this very day. What do you say?"

"I say — rubbish!" said Ratty from the step outside. "Absolute rubbish!"

“Please Ratty,” Toad pleaded. “Do say ‘yes’ and come! I can’t manage without you and it will be such an adventure.”

Ratty looked at Mole and saw at once that he was longing to go. And so, at last, he said slowly, “Oh very well, but don’t blame me if things turn out badly.”

In a surprisingly short time, Toad had harnessed the old horse he kept in the field and they were off!

Toad felt like a king as friendly walkers stopped to admire his outfit, and rabbits sat on their hind legs to watch them pass.

And how pleasant it was when night fell to stop and have supper sitting on the grass by the side of the caravan.

Alas, trouble was not far away. The very next day they were going quietly along the high road, with Mole at the horse's head, when all at once, there was a very loud Poop-poop behind them.

A shining magnificent motor-car rushed past enveloping them in a cloud of choking dust. The horse bucked and reared. Mole was dragged off his feet. Toad finished up sitting in the road. And the caravan landed in the ditch…

The caravan was a complete wreck and the three friends had a long and weary walk to the nearest town. Ratty was so furious with Toad that he wouldn't speak to him. But Toad didn't seem to mind. He talked all the time about the shining motor-car…

Mole couldn't help feeling sorry for Toad and said as much when he and Ratty went out for a spot of fishing the next day. "You needn't bother yourself about Toad," Ratty said crossly. "I got word before we went out — Toad has just ordered himself a very big and expensive, luxury motor-car!"